CHRISTMAS COUPON

TERMS:

CAN BE REDEEMED
ONLY ONCE

GIFTED TO : _____

FROM : _____

CHRISTMAS COUPON

_____

_____

FROM : _____

TO : _____

DATE : _____

EXPIRES : IN 12 MONTHS

TERMS:

CAN BE REDEEMED
ONLY ONCE

CHRISTMAS COUPON

_____

_____

TERMS:

CAN BE REDEEMED
ONLY ONCE

FROM : _____

TO : _____

DATE : _____

EXPIRES : IN 12 MONTHS

CHRISTMAS COUPON

_____

_____

FROM : _____

TO : _____

DATE : _____

EXPIRES : IN 12 MONTHS

TERMS:

CAN BE REDEEMED ONLY ONCE

CHRISTMAS COUPON

_____

_____

FROM : _____

TO : _____

DATE : _____

EXPIRES : IN 12 MONTHS

TERMS:

CAN BE REDEEMED
ONLY ONCE

CHRISTMAS COUPON

_____

_____

FROM : _____

TO : _____

DATE : _____

EXPIRES : IN 12 MONTHS

TERMS:

CAN BE REDEEMED
ONLY ONCE

CHRISTMAS COUPON

_____

_____

FROM : _____

TO : _____

DATE : _____

EXPIRES : IN 12 MONTHS

TERMS:

CAN BE REDEEMED
ONLY ONCE

CHRISTMAS COUPON

_____

_____

TERMS:

CAN BE REDEEMED
ONLY ONCE

FROM : _____

TO : _____

DATE : _____

EXPIRES : IN 12 MONTHS

CHRISTMAS COUPON

_____

_____

FROM : _____

TO : _____

DATE : _____

EXPIRES : IN 12 MONTHS

TERMS:

CAN BE REDEEMED ONLY ONCE

CHRISTMAS COUPON

_____

_____

FROM : _____

TO : _____

DATE : _____

EXPIRES : IN 12 MONTHS

TERMS:

CAN BE REDEEMED ONLY ONCE

CHRISTMAS COUPON

_____

_____

TERMS:

FROM : _____

CAN BE REDEEMED

TO : _____

ONLY ONCE

DATE : _____

EXPIRES : IN 12 MONTHS

CHRISTMAS COUPON

_____

_____

FROM : _____

TO : _____

DATE : _____

EXPIRES : IN 12 MONTHS

TERMS:

CAN BE REDEEMED
ONLY ONCE

CHRISTMAS COUPON

_____

_____

FROM : _____

TO : _____

DATE : _____

EXPIRES : IN 12 MONTHS

TERMS:

CAN BE REDEEMED
ONLY ONCE

CHRISTMAS COUPON

_____

_____

FROM : _____

TO : _____

DATE : _____

EXPIRES : IN 12 MONTHS

TERMS:

CAN BE REDEEMED

ONLY ONCE

CHRISTMAS COUPON

_____

_____

FROM : _____

TO : _____

DATE : _____

EXPIRES : IN 12 MONTHS

TERMS:

CAN BE REDEEMED
ONLY ONCE

CHRISTMAS COUPON

_____

_____

FROM : _____

TO : _____

DATE : _____

EXPIRES : IN 12 MONTHS

TERMS:

CAN BE REDEEMED
ONLY ONCE

CHRISTMAS COUPON

_____

_____

FROM : _____

TO : _____

DATE : _____

EXPIRES : IN 12 MONTHS

TERMS:

CAN BE REDEEMED
ONLY ONCE

CHRISTMAS COUPON

_____

_____

FROM : _____

TO : _____

DATE : _____

EXPIRES : IN 12 MONTHS

TERMS:

CAN BE REDEEMED
ONLY ONCE

CHRISTMAS COUPON

_____

_____

FROM : _____

TO : _____

DATE : _____

EXPIRES : IN 12 MONTHS

TERMS:

CAN BE REDEEMED
ONLY ONCE

CHRISTMAS COUPON

_____

_____

FROM : _____

TO : _____

DATE : _____

EXPIRES : IN 12 MONTHS

TERMS:

CAN BE REDEEMED
ONLY ONCE

CHRISTMAS COUPON

_____

_____

FROM : _____

TO : _____

DATE : _____

EXPIRES : IN 12 MONTHS

TERMS:

CAN BE REDEEMED
ONLY ONCE

CHRISTMAS COUPON

_____

_____

FROM : _____

TO : _____

DATE : _____

EXPIRES : IN 12 MONTHS

TERMS:

CAN BE REDEEMED
ONLY ONCE

CHRISTMAS
COUPON

FROM
TO
DATE
EXPIRES IN 12 MONTHS

TERMS:
CAN BE REDEEMED
ONLY ON

CHRISTMAS COUPON

_____

_____

FROM : _____

TO : _____

DATE : _____

EXPIRES : IN 12 MONTHS

TERMS:

CAN BE REDEEMED

ONLY ONCE

CHRISTMAS COUPON

_____

_____

FROM : _____

TO : _____

DATE : _____

EXPIRES : IN 12 MONTHS

TERMS:

CAN BE REDEEMED
ONLY ONCE

CHRISTMAS
COUPON

FROM
TO
DATE
EXPIRES IN 12 MONTHS

TERMS
FOUR REQUIRED
ONLY ONCE

CHRISTMAS COUPON

_____

_____

FROM : _____

TO : _____

DATE : _____

EXPIRES : IN 12 MONTHS

TERMS:

CAN BE REDEEMED ONLY ONCE

CHRISTMAS COUPON

_____

_____

FROM : _____

TO : _____

DATE : _____

EXPIRES : IN 12 MONTHS

TERMS:

CAN BE REDEEMED

ONLY ONCE

CHRISTMAS COUPON

_____

_____

FROM : _____

TO : _____

DATE : _____

EXPIRES : IN 12 MONTHS

TERMS:

CAN BE REDEEMED
ONLY ONCE

CHRISTMAS COUPON

_____

_____

FROM : _____

TO : _____

DATE : _____

EXPIRES : IN 12 MONTHS

TERMS:

CAN BE REDEEMED ONLY ONCE

CHRISTMAS COUPON

_____

_____

FROM : _____

TO : _____

DATE : _____

EXPIRES : IN 12 MONTHS

TERMS:

CAN BE REDEEMED
ONLY ONCE

CHRISTMAS COUPON

_____

_____

FROM : _____

TO : _____

DATE : _____

EXPIRES : IN 12 MONTHS

TERMS:

CAN BE REDEEMED
ONLY ONCE

CHRISTMAS COUPON

_____

_____

FROM : _____

TO : _____

DATE : _____

EXPIRES : IN 12 MONTHS

TERMS:

CAN BE REDEEMED
ONLY ONCE

CHRISTMAS COUPON

_____

_____

TERMS:

CAN BE REDEEMED
ONLY ONCE

FROM : _____

TO : _____

DATE : _____

EXPIRES : IN 12 MONTHS

CHRISTMAS COUPON

_____

_____

FROM : _____

TO : _____

DATE : _____

EXPIRES : **IN 12 MONTHS**

TERMS:

CAN BE REDEEMED
ONLY ONCE

CHRISTMAS COUPON

_____

_____

FROM : _____

TO : _____

DATE : _____

EXPIRES : IN 12 MONTHS

TERMS:

CAN BE REDEEMED
ONLY ONCE

CHRISTMAS COUPON

TERMS

FROM

TO

DATE

EXPIRES IN 12 MONTHS

CHRISTMAS COUPON

_____

_____

FROM : _____

TO : _____

DATE : _____

EXPIRES : IN 12 MONTHS

TERMS:

CAN BE REDEEMED ONLY ONCE

CHRISTMAS COUPON

_____

_____

FROM : _____

TO : _____

DATE : _____

EXPIRES : IN 12 MONTHS

TERMS:

CAN BE REDEEMED

ONLY ONCE

CHRISTMAS COUPON

_____

_____

FROM : _____

TO : _____

DATE : _____

EXPIRES : IN 12 MONTHS

TERMS:

CAN BE REDEEMED
ONLY ONCE

CHRISTMAS COUPON

_____

_____

FROM : _____

TO : _____

DATE : _____

EXPIRES : IN 12 MONTHS

TERMS:

CAN BE REDEEMED
ONLY ONCE

CHRISTMAS COUPON

_____

_____

FROM : _____

TO : _____

DATE : _____

EXPIRES : IN 12 MONTHS

TERMS:

CAN BE REDEEMED
ONLY ONCE

CHRISTMAS COUPON

_____

_____

FROM : _____

TO : _____

DATE : _____

EXPIRES : IN 12 MONTHS

TERMS:

CAN BE REDEEMED
ONLY ONCE

CHRISTMAS COUPON

_____

_____

FROM : _____

TO : _____

DATE : _____

EXPIRES : IN 12 MONTHS

TERMS:

CAN BE REDEEMED
ONLY ONCE

CHRISTMAS COUPON

_____

_____

FROM : _____

TO : _____

DATE : _____

EXPIRES : IN 12 MONTHS

TERMS:

CAN BE REDEEMED
ONLY ONCE

CHRISTMAS
COUPON

FROM

TO

DATE

EXPIRES in 12 MONTHS

CHRISTMAS COUPON

_____

_____

FROM : _____

TO : _____

DATE : _____

EXPIRES : IN 12 MONTHS

TERMS:

CAN BE REDEEMED
ONLY ONCE

CHRISTMAS COUPON

_____

_____

FROM : _____

TO : _____

DATE : _____

EXPIRES : IN 12 MONTHS

TERMS:

CAN BE REDEEMED

ONLY ONCE

CHRISTMAS COUPON

_____

_____

FROM :_____

TO :_____

DATE :_____

EXPIRES : IN 12 MONTHS

TERMS:

CAN BE REDEEMED
ONLY ONCE

CHRISTMAS COUPON

_____

_____

FROM : _____

TO : _____

DATE : _____

EXPIRES : IN 12 MONTHS

TERMS:

CAN BE REDEEMED

ONLY ONCE

CHRISTMAS
COUPON

FROM

TO

DATE

EXPIRES IN 12 MONTHS

CHRISTMAS COUPON

_____

_____

FROM : _____

TO : _____

DATE : _____

EXPIRES : IN 12 MONTHS

TERMS:

CAN BE REDEEMED
ONLY ONCE

CHRISTMAS COUPON

_____

_____

FROM : _____

TO : _____

DATE : _____

EXPIRES : IN 12 MONTHS

TERMS:

CAN BE REDEEMED ONLY ONCE

CHRISTMAS COUPON

_____

_____

FROM : _____

TO : _____

DATE : _____

EXPIRES : IN 12 MONTHS

TERMS:

CAN BE REDEEMED
ONLY ONCE

CHRISTMAS COUPON

_____

_____

FROM : _____

TO : _____

DATE : _____

EXPIRES : IN 12 MONTHS

TERMS:

CAN BE REDEEMED
ONLY ONCE

CHRISTMAS COUPON

_____

_____

FROM : _____

TO : _____

DATE : _____

EXPIRES : IN 12 MONTHS

TERMS:

CAN BE REDEEMED
ONLY ONCE

CHRISTMAS COUPON

_____

_____

FROM : _____

TO : _____

DATE : _____

EXPIRES : IN 12 MONTHS

TERMS:

CAN BE REDEEMED
ONLY ONCE

CHRISTMAS COUPON

_____

_____

FROM : _____

TO : _____

DATE : _____

EXPIRES : IN 12 MONTHS

TERMS:

CAN BE REDEEMED
ONLY ONCE

CHRISTMAS COUPON

_____

_____

FROM : _____

TO : _____

DATE : _____

EXPIRES : IN 12 MONTHS

TERMS:

CAN BE REDEEMED ONLY ONCE

CHRISTMAS COUPON

_____

_____

FROM : _____

TO : _____

DATE : _____

EXPIRES : IN 12 MONTHS

TERMS:

CAN BE REDEEMED
ONLY ONCE

Made in the USA
Monee, IL
25 October 2024

68665308R00063